To my husband Ken and my children:
Jon, Kate and Allison. You lift me
up, up, up every day! — S. R.

For Mum, for everything — R. O.

Up, Up, Up!

written and sung by Susan Reed

illustrated by Rachel Oldfield

Barefoot Books
Celebrating Art and Story

Up, up, up, up in a balloon.
Up so high I can touch the moon.

Up, up, up, sailing with the clouds.
Look at me! I'm so high, I can fly, I know how.

Trains are fun,
Race cars are fast,

Riding bikes down by the river
Is a blast.

But if I had my way,
Just one chance for a day,

Up, up, up, up in a balloon.
Up so high I can touch the moon.

Up, up, up, sailing with the clouds.
Look at me! I'm so high, I can fly, I know how.

Some creatures swim,
Others climb,

My kind talk all the time.

Up, up, up, up in a balloon.
Up so high I can touch the moon.

Up, up, up, sailing with the clouds.
Look at me! I'm so high, I can fly, I know how.

I feel the rush of the wind
As we climb higher.

I see all people,
All trees,

Cats and dogs,
Bears and monkeys.

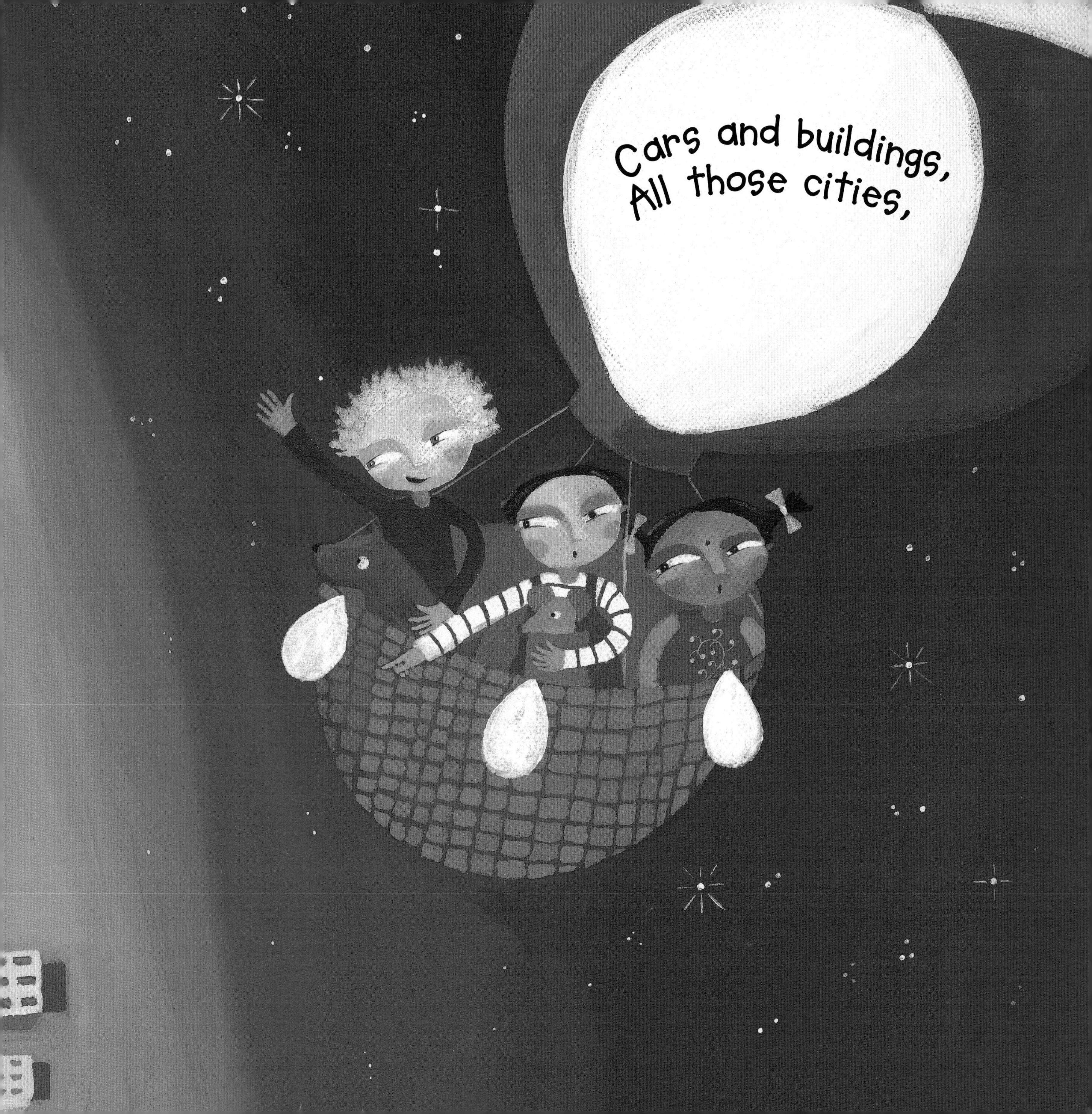

Cars and buildings,
All those cities,

Jungles, mountains and countries.
They're blending into just one color...

And it's green!

I'm headed up, up, up, up in a balloon.
Up so high I can touch the moon.

Up, up, up, sailing with the clouds.
Look at me! I'm so high, I can fly, I know how.

Up, Up, Up!

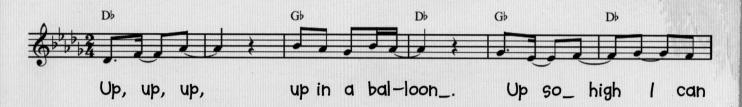

Up, up, up, up in a bal-loon_. Up so_ high I can

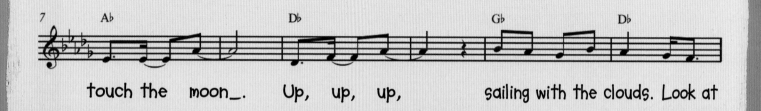

touch the moon_. Up, up, up, sailing with the clouds. Look at

me! I'm so high, I can fly, I know how.

Barefoot Books · 2067 Massachusetts Ave · Cambridge, MA 02140

Text copyright © 2010 by Susan Reed. Illustrations copyright © 2010 by Rachel Oldfield
Music on the accompanying CD written by Susan Reed; performed by Susan Reed, Kate Reed,
Allison Reed, Eric Kilburn and Domenick Fiore. Recorded at Wellspring Sound, Acton, MA
The moral rights of Susan Reed and Rachel Oldfield have been asserted
First published in the United States of America in 2010 by Barefoot Books, Inc. All rights reserved
Printed in China on 100% acid-free paper. Graphic design by Louise Millar, London. Reproduction by B&P International, Hong Kong
This book was typeset in Spumoni and Soupbone. The illustrations were prepared in acrylics

ISBN 978-1-84686-369-1

Library of Congress Cataloging-in-Publication Data is available under LCCN 2009016219

1 3 5 7 9 8 6 4 2

Barefoot Books
Celebrating Art and Story

At Barefoot Books, we celebrate art and story that opens
the hearts and minds of children from all walks of life, inspiring
them to read deeper, search further, and explore their own creative gifts.
Taking our inspiration from many different cultures, we focus on themes that
encourage independence of spirit, enthusiasm for learning, and sharing of
the world's diversity. Interactive, playful and beautiful, our products
combine the best of the present with the best of the past to
educate our children as the caretakers of tomorrow.

Live Barefoot!
Join us at www.barefootbooks.com